SANTA CLAUS
Is Coming to Town

Manufactured in USA.

8 7 6 5 4 3 2 1

ISBN 1-56173-715-1

Contributing writer: Carolyn Quattrocki

Cover illustration: Linda Graves

Book illustrations: Susan Spellman

Publications International, Ltd.

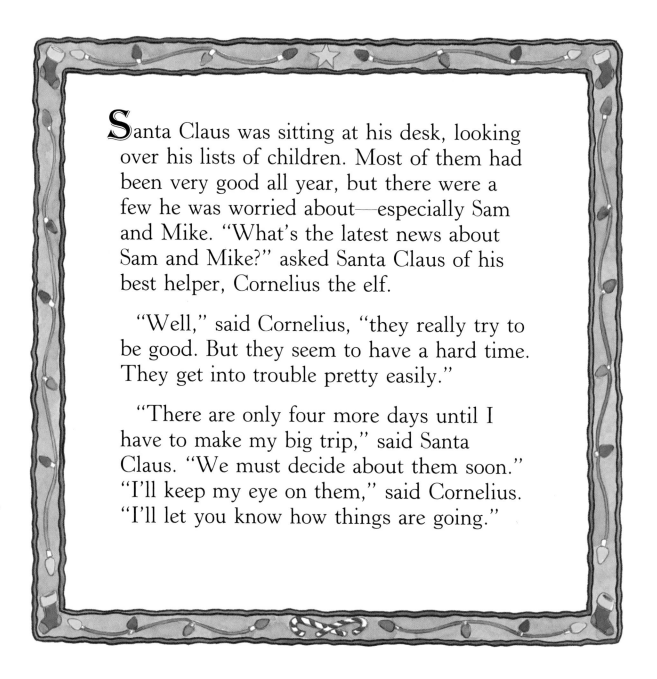

Santa Claus was sitting at his desk, looking over his lists of children. Most of them had been very good all year, but there were a few he was worried about—especially Sam and Mike. "What's the latest news about Sam and Mike?" asked Santa Claus of his best helper, Cornelius the elf.

"Well," said Cornelius, "they really try to be good. But they seem to have a hard time. They get into trouble pretty easily."

"There are only four more days until I have to make my big trip," said Santa Claus. "We must decide about them soon." "I'll keep my eye on them," said Cornelius. "I'll let you know how things are going."

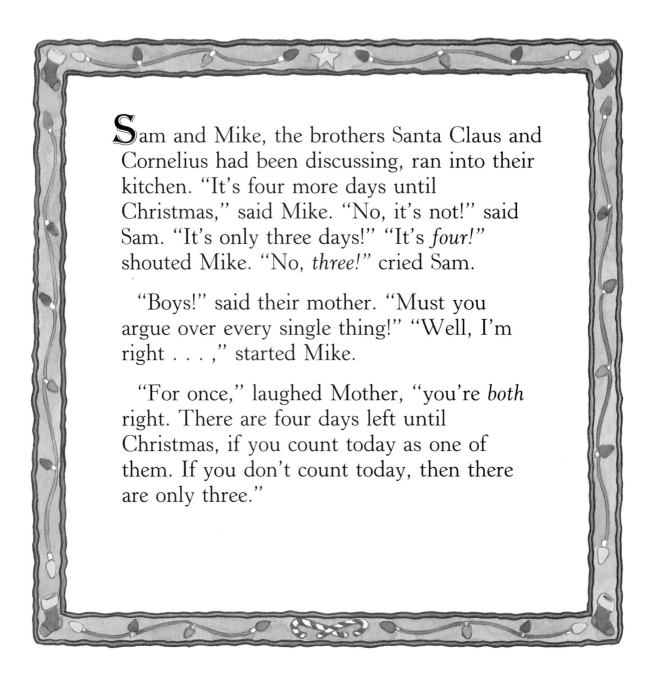

Sam and Mike, the brothers Santa Claus and Cornelius had been discussing, ran into their kitchen. "It's four more days until Christmas," said Mike. "No, it's not!" said Sam. "It's only three days!" "It's *four!*" shouted Mike. "No, *three!*" cried Sam.

"Boys!" said their mother. "Must you argue over every single thing!" "Well, I'm right . . . ," started Mike.

"For once," laughed Mother, "you're *both* right. There are four days left until Christmas, if you count today as one of them. If you don't count today, then there are only three."

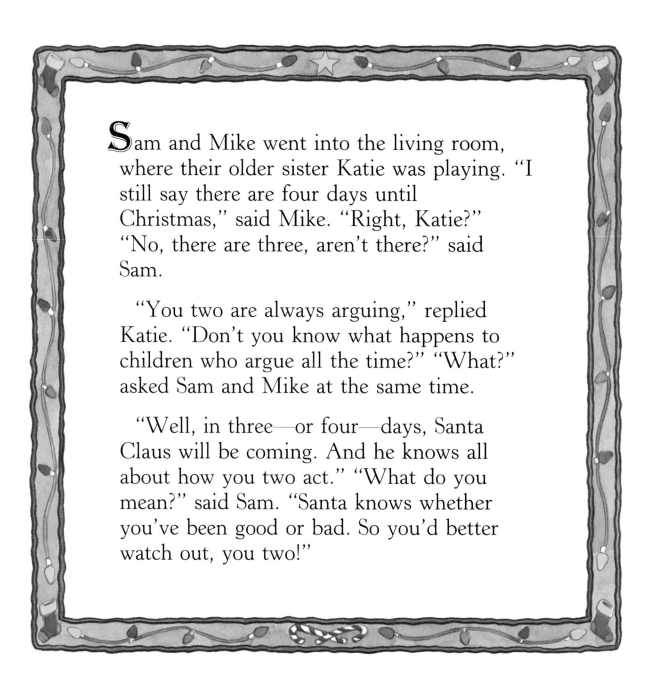

Sam and Mike went into the living room, where their older sister Katie was playing. "I still say there are four days until Christmas," said Mike. "Right, Katie?" "No, there are three, aren't there?" said Sam.

"You two are always arguing," replied Katie. "Don't you know what happens to children who argue all the time?" "What?" asked Sam and Mike at the same time.

"Well, in three—or four—days, Santa Claus will be coming. And he knows all about how you two act." "What do you mean?" said Sam. "Santa knows whether you've been good or bad. So you'd better watch out, you two!"

"Gee!" said Mike. "Maybe we *should* be careful. Okay, no more arguments. Let's go sledding." Sam and Mike ran to the closet to get their coats and boots. "Last one outside is a . . . ! Oops, I forgot," said Sam.

Walking down the street, they passed Mr. Paulson's yard. "That's the best hill for sledding," said Mike. "Let's try to sneak in and sled down just once." "Mr. Paulson said he doesn't want anyone to sled in his yard," replied Sam. "But maybe just this one time wouldn't hurt."

But just as they were pushing their sleds off from the top of the hill, who should look out the window but Mr. Paulson. "What did I tell you boys!" he shouted from his door, waving his fist.

Meanwhile, Santa Claus decided to see how things were going in his workshop. The elves were working furiously. "Cornelius," called out Santa, "what's the latest news on those two mischief-makers, Sam and Mike?"

Cornelius shook his head and told Santa about Sam and Mike's argument. He also said they had gone sledding in Mr. Paulson's yard. "Those boys," said Santa Claus sadly. "They do have a hard time being good. What do they want for Christmas?"

Cornelius and another elf held up two toys. "Mike wants a toy train like this one, and Sam would like some ice skates," said Cornelius. "Well, I sure hope I'll be able to deliver them," said Santa.

It was just about this time that Sam and Mike were continuing on their way toward the park. "Maybe we'll find something fun to do there without getting into trouble," said Mike.

Sam and Mike finally got to the park. There they found a group of boys building snow forts. The boys had chosen teams and were going to see who could build the biggest and best snow fort. Then they'd have a snowball fight.

"Let us help," called Mike and Sam. "Sure, join in," said Charlie, one of the bigger boys. Just then, Sam noticed a little boy sitting by a tree, away from the other boys. It was Joey. He looked like he had been crying.

"What's wrong with Joey?" Mike asked Charlie. "Oh, Joey wanted to be on one of our teams," said Charlie. "But he's too little." Sam and Mike thought about that and decided they didn't agree. "Hey, Joey!" called Sam. "Mike and I need someone just your size to reach the tough spots."

The three of them got to work. Soon their fort was as tall as the other ones. And then, with Mike and Sam lifting Joey up high to pile the snow on top, their fort stood even taller!

"Joey," called Charlie. "Would you help our team a second? We need to reach up to the high spots, too." With a big smile, Joey ran over to help Charlie's team.

A few days later, at the North Pole, Santa Claus was getting ready for his trip. The time had finally arrived—it was Christmas Eve! Santa had already hitched up his reindeer. "Cornelius," called Santa, "what is the latest news on Sam and Mike? I'm ready to pack their skates and train."

"Great news, Santa," said Cornelius. Then he told Santa Claus all about how Sam and Mike had asked Joey to help them build their snow fort, when none of the other boys would let Joey play.

Santa smiled his biggest smile of the day. "I *knew* they were good boys!" he exclaimed. "Sam and Mike did the most important thing—they were kind to another person. That's what really counts."

As Santa Claus was starting on his trip, his sleigh loaded with toys, Sam and Mike were getting ready for bed. They had hung up their stockings by the chimney. Cookies and milk were carefully set out in case Santa wanted a snack.

After they were all tucked into bed, Mike whispered, "Hey, Sam, look out!" Just then, he threw his pillow across the room. It landed on Sam's head. With a whoop, Sam yelled, "I'll get *you!*" He started to throw his own pillow back at Mike. But then he thought, "*Someone* knows whether I'm being good or not."

At that same moment, Mike remembered that *someone* knew when he was sleeping and when he was awake.

Mike just whispered, "Good night, Sam, and Merry Christmas!" A hush fell over the room as they closed their eyes.

Late that night, while Mike and Sam slept, a smiling Santa put a little toy train and some shiny new ice skates carefully under the tree. If they had been awake, they would have heard a happy Santa say, "Well done, Mike and Sam! You were good, for goodness sake!"